MW01065337

CAREER EXPLORATION

# Computer Engineer

by Melissa Maupin

**Consultant:**
Dr. Phillip A. Laplante, President
Pennsylvania Institute of Technology

## CAPSTONE BOOKS

an imprint of Capstone Press
Mankato, Minnesota

Capstone Books are published by Capstone Press
151 Good Counsel Drive, P.O. Box 669, Mankato, Minnesota 56002
http://www.capstone-press.com

*Library of Congress Cataloging-in-Publication Data*
Maupin, Melissa, 1958–
    Computer engineer/by Melissa Maupin.
    p. cm.—(Career exploration)
    Includes bibliographical references and index.
    Summary: Introduces the career of computer engineer, providing information
about educational requirements, duties, the workplace, salary, employment outlook,
and possible future positions.
    ISBN 0-7368-0591-5
    1. Computer science—Vocational guidance—Juvenile literature. 2. Computer
engineering—Vocational guidance—Juvenile literature. [1. Computer science—
Vocational guidance. 2. Computer engineering—Vocational guidance. 3. Vocational
guidance.] I. Title. II. Series.

QA76.25. M38 2001
004'.023'73—dc21                                                      00-023740

**Editorial Credits**
Connie R. Colwell, editor; Steve Christensen, cover designer; Kia Bielke, production
    designer and illustrator; Heidi Schoof and Kimberly Danger, photo researchers

**Photo Credits**
Diane Meyer, 20
Hewlett-Packard, cover, 6, 30, 32
Index Stock Imagery, 34
International Stock/Tom Carroll, 12; Mark Gibson, 26
John Zioner/Pictor, 14
Leslie O'Shaughnessy, 24, 38
Llewellyn/Pictor, 40, 43
Melanie Carr/Pictor, 19
The Photographers' Library/Pictor, 16
Unicorn Stock Photos/Nancy Ferguson, 9; Rod Furgason, 10
Warren Faidley, 23

1  2  3  4  5  6  06  05  04  03  02  01

# Table of Contents

# Fast Facts

| | |
|---|---|
| **Career Title** | Computer Engineer |
| **O*NET Number** | 22127 |
| **DOT Cluster**<br>(Dictionary of Occupational Titles) | Professional, technical, and managerial occupations |
| **DOT Number** | 030.062-010/033.167-010 |
| **GOE Number**<br>(Guide for Occupational Exploration) | 05.01.03/11.01.01 |
| **NOC Number**<br>(National Occupational Classification-Canada) | 214/2163 |
| **Salary Range**<br>(U.S. Bureau of Labor Statistics and Human Resources Development Canada, late 1990s figures) | U.S.: $39,722 to $63,367<br>Canada: $28,200 to $67,700<br>(Canadian dollars) |
| **Minimum Educational Requirements** | U.S.: bachelor's degree<br>Canada: bachelor's degree |
| **Certification/Licensing Requirements** | U.S.: optional<br>Canada: varies by province |

| | |
|---|---|
| **Subject Knowledge** | Administration and management; computers and electronics; engineering and technology; design; math; English language; telecommunications |
| **Personal Abilities/Skills** | Use high level math, advanced logic, and scientific thinking to solve complex problems; use computer technology to solve problems; speak and write clearly and accurately; use technical terms, mathematical and computer symbols, and complex charts and graphs; understand principles of science; solve problems using facts and personal judgment |
| **Job Outlook** | U.S.: faster than average growth Canada: good |
| **Personal Interests** | Mechanical: interest in applying mechanical principles to practical situations |
| **Similar Types of Jobs** | Computer programmer; computer scientist; systems analyst; financial analyst; statistician; mathematician |

# Chapter 1

# Computer Engineer

Computer engineers design computers and the programs that run them. They also solve problems with existing computers and programs.

A computer's outside and inside parts are called hardware. Computer programs are called software. Computer engineers who design the parts of computers are called computer hardware engineers. Computer engineers who design software are called software engineers. Software engineers also are called computer programmers.

Computer engineers improve computer designs. They develop ways to make computers run faster and more smoothly.

**Computers' outside parts are called hardware.**

They design new types of computers and software to perform different tasks. They also search for new ways to use computers.

## Designing Computers

Many computer engineers work for companies that make computers, computer parts, or software. Computer hardware engineers at these companies design the inside and outside parts of computers. These engineers also design peripherals. People connect these devices to their computers to help them perform tasks. Peripherals include printers, monitors, and modems. Modems are electronic devices that use telephone lines or cable systems to send information between computers.

Software engineers at computer companies design software that runs computers. Software engineers load this software onto computers before the computers are sold. They also design software that computer users can add to their computers later.

Both computer hardware and software engineers also may work for companies that

**Software engineers design software that computer users add to their computers.**

make microchips. These tiny pieces of silicon are placed inside computers. Microchips have electronic circuits etched or printed on them. These circuits instruct computers to perform certain tasks. Computer hardware engineers design and build the circuits. Software engineers program the chips with memory. Computers use memory to run their systems.

**Monitors are computer peripherals.**

## Other Opportunities

Computer engineers may work in other settings. They may design computers and software for large companies. They may work for hospitals or universities. Computer engineers also may work for the military or government agencies.

Computer hardware engineers at these places study the organization's computer needs. The engineers find computers, peripherals, and software that fit the organization's needs. They advise the organization to purchase the selected computer hardware or software. They then may design computer systems with these parts. These engineers also may be in charge of solving problems with the computer systems.

Some software engineers work as independent contractors. These engineers work for themselves or with a group of software engineers. Businesses hire the engineers to design software systems. Software engineers who work as independent contractors may work for several companies each year.

## The Workplace

Computer engineers usually work in teams. Team members may be other computer engineers. They also may be employees who work in marketing or manufacturing departments. Each team member shares ideas and information about a project. Team members work together to create new computers, computer parts, or software.

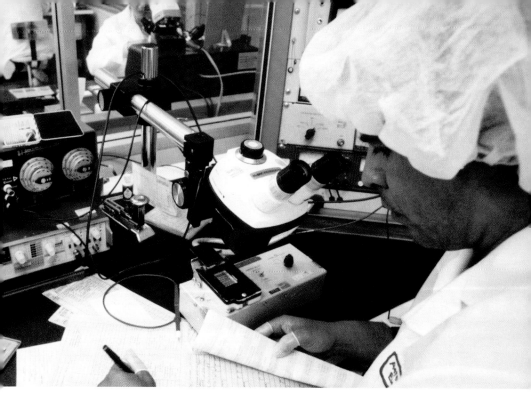

**Engineers at microchip manufacturing companies often work in clean rooms.**

Some computer engineers work in laboratories. These rooms have special equipment that engineers use to test computer designs. Computer engineers compare their designs to others on the market to see which designs work best. They also test the hardware and software to find bugs. These errors in the hardware and software cause computers to run incorrectly.

Engineers at microchip manufacturing companies often work in clean rooms. These rooms are controlled to keep out dirt and dust. Even one speck of dust can harm microchips. The engineers must wear special suits that completely cover their bodies. They often must wear hoods with air tanks to keep the air clean.

Computer engineers may telecommute. These engineers use personal computers to design hardware and software from their homes or offices in other locations. They then use modems to send their designs or other information to their workplaces.

## Tools and Skills

Computer engineers use computers and software to perform their work. They use computer programs to write proposals. These plans suggest their project ideas to others. Computer engineers use software to make charts and graphs describing their projects. They produce schematics of their designs on

computers. These detailed descriptions and drawings help others understand their designs.

Hardware engineers use computer programs to draw plans and blueprints for their products. Blueprints are detailed plans for a project or idea. Engineers create plans using Computer-Aided Design (CAD) software. This software allows engineers to produce computer models of their designs. They can see how the designs will look when they are produced. Engineers then can change their designs quickly and inexpensively.

Software engineers use computers to design new software programs. They use computer languages to write the programs. These languages include C, Visual Basic, and Java. Computer engineers usually know which of the many computer languages works best for each project. Software engineers also test existing software on computers. They study the software and design ways to improve it.

**Software engineers often test existing software on computers.**

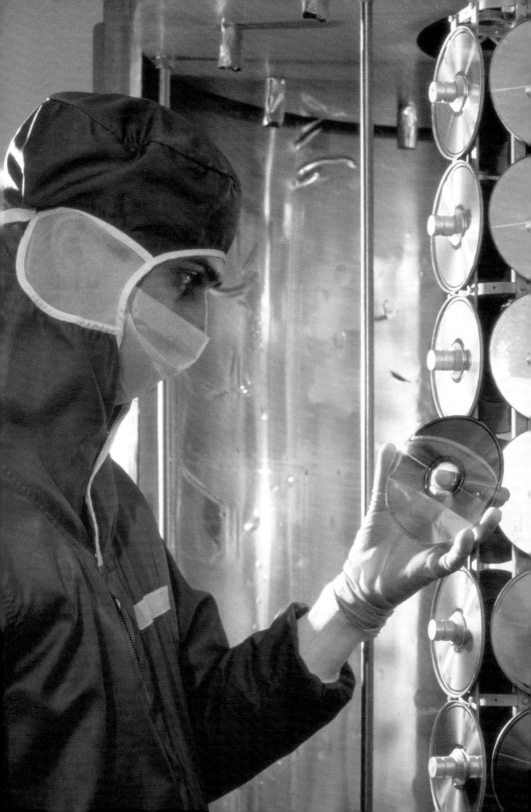

# Chapter 2

# Day-to-Day Activities

Computer engineers' daily activities vary depending on their jobs. They may have one important project to work on for a long period of time. They also may have several smaller projects to complete in one day.

## Beginning a Project

Computer engineers must determine the needs of each client. These people or companies use the services of computer engineers. Engineers work with team members to create hardware or software systems that meet the clients' needs.

**Computer engineers' daily activities vary depending on their jobs.**

They sometimes must create new methods or products to solve clients' problems.

Team members may have certain requirements for projects. They usually have a budget for each project. Engineers must follow this plan for spending money as they work on the project. Team members also must meet the project's deadline. This is the date when the project must be completed.

Computer hardware engineers begin a project by meeting with other project team members. The members discuss the project's purpose. The purpose may be to design computers for people to use at home or in schools. It may be to create a computer that operates machines in a factory.

Computer hardware engineers may work with product designers. These designers help engineers make decisions about how the outside of the computer will look. Designers make computer products that will appeal to users. Engineers consider the computer's function as they design its size and shape.

**Computer engineers may need to create a computer system for business workers.**

Software engineers usually begin their projects with a set of specifications. These detailed written plans tell the engineers what the clients need from a software system. Software engineers who work as independent contractors may meet with clients to discuss the clients' needs.

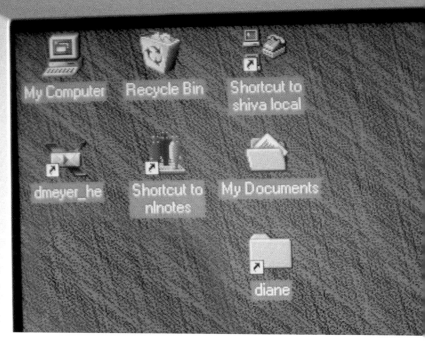

**Software engineers decide which icons to use in computer programs.**

## Designing the Product

Computer hardware engineers design computers after the plans and meetings are completed. They decide how the electrical current will run through the machine. Electricity flows along the current. Engineers design the size, structure, and placement of the electronic circuit boards. These devices connect the chips inside a computer. Computer hardware engineers also design the central processing unit (CPU). The CPU processes all the computer's commands.

Computer hardware engineers draw their designs using CAD programs. They may share the design work with other hardware engineers. Engineers then send the plans to the other team members. These plans may be in the form of paper or electronic files. The members review the designs and send back suggestions or changes.

Software engineers must consider many things while they design software systems. They must consider the software's purpose. Software engineers design menus, task bars, and tool bars that their clients can use. They also design simple ways for clients to switch from one program to another. Software engineers consider the design of the screens in the program. They decide which icons to use. These small figures represent functions programs can perform. Software engineers also decide how to arrange the icons on the program's screens.

Software engineers then share their designs with team members and clients. Team members may make suggestions to improve the software. Clients may ask to add features or make changes to the software.

## Testing the Product

Computer hardware engineers and team members build a model of the computer or part. Engineers design the model to look like the finished product. But the model's parts do not function. The model allows the team members to see how the parts of the product will fit together.

Technicians then build prototypes of the computer hardware. These versions of the product allow team members to see how the product will look and work. Technicians use the engineers' plans as a guide as they build prototypes.

Many people test the prototypes before the product is manufactured. They test the prototypes by using them in various ways. Marketing employees use prototypes to determine if people will buy the products.

**Technicians use engineers' plans as a guide when they build prototypes.**

Manufacturing employees review the prototypes to see if the products will meet the set budget. Software engineers test the computer hardware by programming it to run software. They make sure the computer and the software work properly together.

Software engineers also make prototypes of their designs. They test software by using the

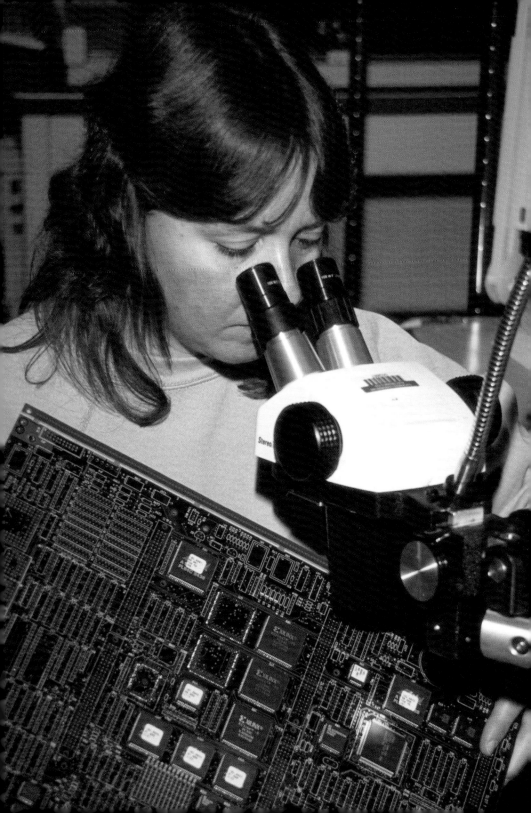

programs on computers. Software engineers also may ask team members to use the software. Team members may suggest ways to fix any bugs or other problems.

Both computer hardware and software engineers then make notes about any prototype problems. They discuss what may be causing the problems. Computer hardware engineers may have to redesign the computer hardware to correct the problems. They may abandon some designs. Engineers continue to test prototypes until the team approves the designs.

Companies manufacture the computer hardware and software after the designs are approved. Engineers may work with manufacturing department employees to solve any manufacturing problems. Engineers also help write instructions and specifications about the products. Customers need this information to properly use the products.

**Companies manufacture the computer hardware and software when the designs are approved.**

# Chapter 3

# The Right Candidate

Computer engineers need a variety of skills and abilities. They need strong math and computer skills. Computer engineers need good communication skills. They also must be willing to learn about new technology.

## Interests

People interested in computer engineering usually have a strong interest in technology. They may enjoy reading technical or computer books and magazines. They should be interested in learning about advances in technology. They should want to learn new programs and computer skills.

People interested in computer engineering should have a strong interest in technology.

# Skills

## Workplace Skills                                        Yes / No

### Resources:
Assign use of time ................................... ☑ ❑
Assign use of money ................................. ☑ ❑
Assign use of material and facility resources .............. ☑ ❑
Assign use of human resources ....................... ☑ ❑

### Interpersonal Skills:
Take part as a member of a team ..................... ☑ ❑
Teach others ........................................ ☑ ❑
Serve clients/customers .............................. ☑ ❑
Show leadership ..................................... ☑ ❑
Work with others to arrive at a decision .............. ☑ ❑
Work with a variety of people ........................ ☑ ❑

### Information:
Acquire and judge information ........................ ☑ ❑
Understand and follow legal requirements .............. ☑ ❑
Organize and maintain information .................... ☑ ❑
Understand and communicate information .............. ☑ ❑
Use computers to process information ................. ☑ ❑

### Systems:
Identify, understand, and work with systems ........... ☑ ❑
Understand environmental, social, political, economic,
        or business systems ........................... ☑ ❑
Oversee and correct system performance .............. ☑ ❑
Improve and create systems .......................... ☑ ❑

### Technology:
Select technology ................................... ☑ ❑
Apply technology to task ............................ ☑ ❑
Maintain and troubleshoot technology ................ ☑ ❑

## Foundation Skills

### Basic Skills:
Read ............................................... ☑ ❑
Write .............................................. ☑ ❑
Do arithmetic and math ............................. ☑ ❑
Speak and listen ................................... ☑ ❑

### Thinking Skills:
Learn .............................................. ☑ ❑
Reason ............................................. ☑ ❑
Think creatively ................................... ☑ ❑
Make decisions ..................................... ☑ ❑
Solve problems ..................................... ☑ ❑

### Personal Qualities:
Take individual responsibility ....................... ☑ ❑
Have self-esteem and self-management ................ ☑ ❑
Be sociable ........................................ ☑ ❑
Be fair, honest, and sincere ......................... ☑ ❑

People interested in hardware engineering usually have a strong interest in machines and electronics. They may take apart machines to discover how they work. They also may build electronic equipment or repair computers as a hobby.

People who want to be software engineers usually can operate a variety of software programs. They may write simple programs. They also may play computer games.

## Skills and Abilities

Computer engineers should have excellent math skills. Computer engineers use math to solve many computer design problems. They should be able to understand and use mathematical symbols and formulas.

Computer engineers must be able to solve problems quickly and creatively. They often work on difficult problems. They must use their judgment to solve these problems.

Communication skills are important in computer engineering. Computer engineers must explain their plans for projects in detailed written reports. Computer engineers also need effective public speaking skills in order to present projects to team members or clients.

# Chapter 4

# Preparing for the Career

People interested in becoming computer engineers must prepare for the career. This preparation includes both education and training.

## High School Education

Students interested in computer engineering need a strong background in math and science. They should take math classes such as algebra, geometry, and calculus. They also should take advanced science classes such as chemistry and physics.

Students who want to be computer engineers should take communications classes. English

**Computer engineers must earn a bachelor's degree from a college or university.**

**Students interested in computer engineering should take math classes.**

classes help students learn to write effectively. Speech classes help students communicate their ideas to others.

High school students interested in computer engineering should take computer classes. These classes might include computer science, keyboarding, or desktop publishing. Students learn to design books, magazines, and other documents in desktop publishing courses.

Programming classes are especially helpful. Students study computer languages and write simple programs in these classes.

High school students may benefit by joining school or community computer clubs. These clubs help students learn about computers. Computer clubs also may sponsor scholarships. Students use these money awards to help pay for college costs.

High school students may find part-time or summer jobs in the computer field. Students may be data entry workers for businesses or companies. These workers use keyboards to enter data into computers. Students also may work for web design businesses. These businesses design Internet sites for clients. Some high school students even have their own software or web page design businesses.

## Post-Secondary Education

Computer engineers must earn a bachelor's degree from a college or university. Students can complete these degrees in about four years. Most computer hardware engineers earn

**Many computer hardware engineers earn college degrees in computer science.**

degrees in computer science, computer engineering, or electrical engineering. Most software engineers earn degrees in computer science, computer engineering, or math.

Computer engineering students take a variety of classes. These include science, math, and English classes. Students also take a variety of computer classes. These include computer programming and theory classes. Students learn the rules and principles of computer engineering in theory classes.

Employers often prefer to hire college graduates who have experience in the computer field. Students can gain experience from part-time or summer jobs. College students also may work as interns. Interns receive college credit for working at computer companies or businesses. Some interns also receive a salary. Many students work as interns during their last year of college or the year after they graduate.

Many computer engineers go on to obtain advanced degrees. Many earn a master's degree. Some engineers earn a doctoral degree. These are the highest degrees available from universities. Computer engineers study and research a particular area of computer engineering in order to earn a master's or doctoral degree.

## Certification

In the United States, computer engineers do not need to be certified. But many employees prefer to hire engineers who are certified. Some companies that sell computer products hire only

**High
School
Diploma**

**Bachelor's
Degree**

certified engineers. Certification proves that computer engineers are qualified for their jobs.

In Canada, some employers require computer engineers to be certified as Professional Engineers (PEs). Provincial or territorial associations provide these certifications. Computer engineers in Quebec must get PE certification. These engineers must pass exams and register with an association of professional engineers.

Two professional organizations offer certification. These groups are the Institute for Certification of Computing Professionals and the Quality Assurance Institute. Students must pass exams to become certified. They also must have work experience in a computer field.

**Certification**      **Advanced Degree**

## Continuing Education

Technology changes very quickly. Computer engineers must continue to learn about their field throughout their career.

Employers often train their employees to help them keep current with trends in technology. Many computer companies offer training seminars for engineers. Some of these companies may even help engineers earn professional certification. Professional computer groups sometimes offer classes and training for engineers.

Many computer engineers continue to learn about the field in college or university classes. Some take classes to learn about new technology. Others earn a master's or doctoral degree in computer engineering or a related field.

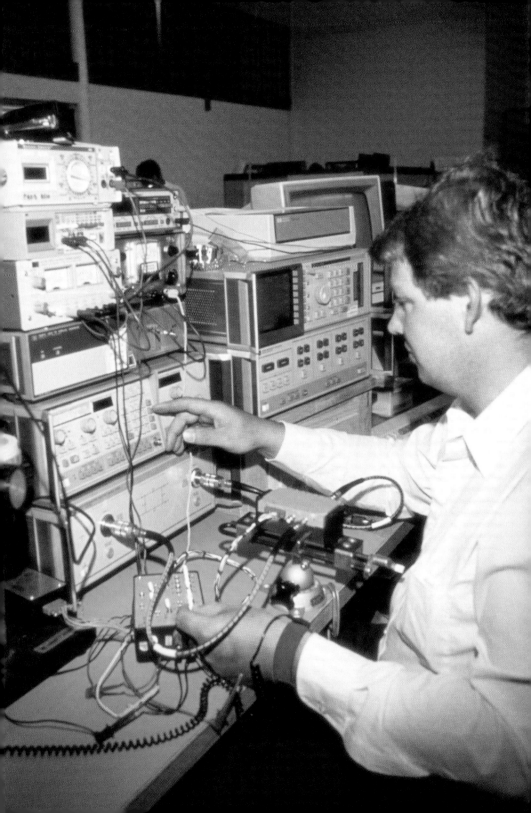

# Chapter 5

# The Market

The job market for computer engineers is excellent. The rapid increase in technology during the last 20 years has created a need for highly trained workers. Rapid growth in technology is predicted to continue into the future. This growth will mean more job openings for computer engineers.

## Salary

Computer engineers' salaries vary with their level of education. Certified engineers or those with more experience also may earn higher salaries than non-certified engineers.

In the United States, most computer engineers earn between $39,722 and $63,367

**The job market for computer engineers is excellent.**

**Engineers with recent training earn higher salaries.**

per year. The average computer engineer salary is $43,940.

In Canada, computer engineers' annual salaries range from $28,200 to $67,700. The average salary is $46,900.

## Job Outlook

Computer services will continue to grow in the future. In the United States, computer engineering is expected to be one of the fastest growing occupations. In Canada, opportunities for computer engineers are expected to be good. Most new computer engineering jobs in Canada are expected to occur in professional and business services.

Computer hardware and software will continue to improve and become more specialized. Hardware and software also will continue to become more affordable. More people will be able to purchase these items. For these reasons, many businesses will expand their computer systems. They will need computer hardware engineers to build systems for them and help them select the right systems. They will need software engineers to design and set up new software systems.

## Advancement Opportunities

Computer engineers may advance in their field by continuing their education and training. Engineers with higher degrees and recent training earn higher salaries. They also may secure more favorable job positions.

Experienced computer engineers also may advance to better positions as they gain experience. Experienced computer engineers may work as team leaders. Team leaders oversee projects from beginning to end. Engineers may be able to move up into management positions after working for several years.

Some software engineers work for themselves as independent contractors. Others start their own software firms. Self-employed engineers take a greater risk in the business world. But they also have more flexibility in their work schedules. Self-employed software engineers also may earn higher than average salaries.

## Related Careers

People interested in computers may be able to find jobs in related careers. Some people work as computer scientists. Computer scientists perform research and experiments in order to expand computer technology. They may invent new technologies or computer languages.

People may become database administrators. A database is a group of computer files that organizes and stores information. Database administrators design and set up databases. They monitor the systems for problems and fix any problems that occur.

Some people work as systems analysts. Systems analysts set up entire computer software and hardware systems. They may maintain the

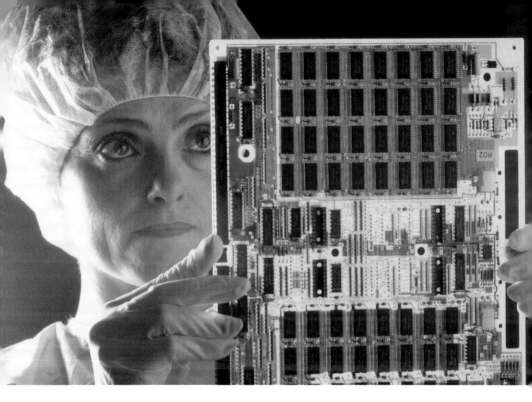

**The computer industry is growing and changing.**

systems so they work properly. They also update old systems. They usually specialize in designing one type of system. Analysts may specialize in designing systems for business, science, or engineering.

The computer industry is growing and changing. As it grows, new jobs will continue to develop. Computer engineers who keep current with technology will be needed to meet the demand.

# Words to Know

**database** (DAY-tuh-bayss)—a group of computer files that organizes and stores information

**hardware** (HARD-wair)— computer equipment; hardware includes internal parts of a computer as well as printers, monitors, or keyboards.

**microchip** (MYE-kroh-chip)—a tiny piece of silicon that contains etched electronic circuits

**peripheral** (puh-RIF-ur-uhl)—a device that connects to a computer and allows a user to perform additional functions; peripherals include printers, monitors, and modems.

**prototype** (PROH-tuh-tipe)—a model of a design

**software** (SAWFT-wair)—computer programs that control the working of the equipment or hardware and direct it to do specific tasks

# To Learn More

**Basta, Nicholas.** *Careers in High Tech.* VGM Professional Careers. Lincolnwood, Ill.: VGM Career Horizons, 1999.

**Cosgrove, Holli, ed.** *Career Discovery Encyclopedia.* Vols. 4 and 7. Chicago: Ferguson Publishing, 2000.

**Farr, J. Michael, and LaVerne L. Ludden, eds.** *Best Jobs for the 21st Century.* Indianapolis: JIST Works, Inc., 1999.

**Garner, Geraldine O.** *Great Jobs for Engineering Majors.* Lincolnwood, Ill.: VGM Career Horizons, 1996.

*Peterson's Job Opportunities for Engineering and Computer Science Majors.* Princeton, N.J.: Peterson's, 1998.

# Useful Addresses

**Association for Computing Machinery**
1515 Broadway
New York, NY  10036

**Association for Women in Computing (AWC)**
41 Sutter Street
Suite 1006
San Francisco, CA  94104

**Canadian Society for Computational Studies
of Intelligence (CSCSI)**
CIPS National Office
One Yonge Street
Suite 2401
Toronto, ON  M5E 1E5
Canada

**IEEE Computer Society**
Headquarters Office
1730 Massachusetts Avenue NW
Washington, DC  20036

# Internet Sites

**Association for Computing Machinery**
http://info.acm.org

**Job Futures—Other Engineers**
http://www.hrdc-drhc.gc.ca/corp/stratpol/arb/
    jobs/english/volume1/214/214.htm

**MainFunction**
http://www.mainfunction.com

**Occupational Outlook Handbook—**
    **Computer Systems Analysts, Engineers,**
    **and Scientists**
http://stats.bls.gov/oco/ocos042.htm

# Index